All Eyes on
ALEXANDRA

For Kol —A.L.

To my family of cranes: Anna, Giangiorgio, Gaia, and Luca —C.P.

Thank you to photographer Aviran Avizedeq, and to Alen Kacal of the Jerusalem Bird Observatory —A.L.

KAR-BEN PUBLISHING, INC.
A division of Lerner Publishing Group, Inc.
241 First Avenue North
Minneapolis, MN 55401 USA
1-800-4-KARBEN

Website address: www.karben.com

Main body text set in ITC Slimbach Std 15/21.
Typeface provided by Adobe Systems.

Library of Congress Cataloging-in-Publication Data

Names: Levine, Anna (Anna Yaphe), author. | Pasqualotto,
   Chiara, illustrator.
Title: All eyes on Alexandra / by Anna Levine ; illustrated by
   Chiara Pasqualotto.
Description: Minneapolis : Kar-Ben Publishing, [2018] | Series:
   Hanukkah | Summary: While preparing for a long migration,
   Alexandra Crane's family is concerned that she prefers
   wandering to staying in formation, but all are surprised when she
   proves an excellent leader.
Identifiers: LCCN 2017030087| ISBN 9781512444407 (pb) |
   ISBN 9781541500488 (eb pdf)
Subjects: | CYAC: Individuality—Fiction. | Leadership—Fiction. | Cranes
   (Birds)—Fiction. | Birds—Migration—Fiction.
Classification: LCC PZ7.L57823 All 2018 | DDC [E]—dc23

LC record available at https://lccn.loc.gov/2017030087

Manufactured in the United States of America
1-42512-26189-11/22/2017

All Eyes on
ALEXANDRA

Anna Levine   illustrations by Chiara Pasqualotto

KAR-BEN
PUBLISHING

Alexandra Crane had her head in the clouds.

"Stay with the Vee, Alexandra," called Abba Crane. The Crane family was out on a morning spin, practicing their hovers and glides. Soon they would set off for Israel. It was almost time for their winter visit before flying to their summer home in Africa.

"She refuses to follow," her brothers honked.

"She soars when we dip," said her sisters.

"Even when we're on land, her head doesn't follow her feet," said her cousins, as they tried to teach her to march.

Alexandra didn't mean to be difficult.
She loved to flap and fly with her family,
but lately, she had an urge to wander.

There were volcanoes to inspect and rushing waterfalls to splash in.

"Oh Alexandra," sighed Ima Crane. "We can't have you getting lost. The world is a difficult place to navigate all on your own."

With her head held high and beak stretched forward, Alexandra sniffed the air. "I'm sensing snow," she said.

"She's right," said Saba Crane. "It's time to be on our way to Israel, where the winds are warm and the sun shines bright."

The Crane family cheered.

"Now, Alexandra," Ima Crane went on,
"We all have to stay close and follow behind."

"I'll try," said Alexandra.

"You have to admit," said Saba Crane,
"Alexandra is never afraid to try new things."

"But what will we do if she falls behind?"
Ima Crane worried. "We can't leave her on
her own in Europe all winter."

"I'd manage," said Alexandra with a smile.

"We're birds of a feather, and flocks stay together," said Abba.
"We'll just have to keep all eyes on Alexandra."

The Cranes prepared for their long journey. The uncles cleaned their coats. The aunties dyed their hair from red to brown to blend better with the winter foliage. The cousins, wanting to look debonair, greased back each feather with care.

Meanwhile, Saba Crane took Alexandra aside. "Let's practice," he said. "Follow me."

Alexandra caught a glide on a warm thermal current and soared on ahead.
"Look, Saba! Mountain peaks. Oh my—and danger, too."

"Where?" said Saba in alarm, dipping lower to see.

"There!" cried Alexandra as a greater spotted eagle swooped toward them with her sharp beak and claws. "Quick! Let's get out of here!"

Flapping their wings with all their might, Saba and Alexandra dove and weaved, outsmarting the eagle until finally it was barely a dot in the sky.

"That was close!" said Saba, gasping for breath. "Well done, Alexandra. Now I think it's time to head home." He looked around at the unfamiliar landscape.

"This way," said Alexandra.

Saba Crane hesitated. "Are you sure?"

"Absolutely," said Alexandra. "I've been studying the wind and thermal currents. Follow me."

Alexandra and Saba Crane returned home just as the rest of the Cranes were ready to leave on their winter journey to Israel.

"Stay close," said Abba to the family. "We have a long flight ahead of us."

Up, up, up the flock flew, with
Saba in the lead.

When Saba got tired, he dropped to
the back of the Vee and let Abba take
over. Then Savta soared to the front.

"I'm ready for a break!" Savta called.
"Who's going to lead next?"

"I think it should be
Alexandra," said Saba,
to everyone's surprise.

"Are you sure?" asked Ima Crane.

"Absolutely! She may not like to follow, but Alexandra sure knows how to lead. She's not afraid to try new routes. She's got a sharp eye for danger. And she never gives up until she finds the best way."

Alexandra beamed. "And with me in the lead, we'll have time for a little exploring!"

They sailed over Syria and flew above Lebanon . . .

. . . until they landed in Israel, where
they hitched a ride on the cable car at
Rosh Hanikra . . .

. . . and took a detour west for a
dip in the Mediterranean Sea . . .

. . . played water tag in the falls at Ein Gedi . . .

. . . and stopped for a drink by the shore of the Kinneret.

Finally Alexandra led the flock to the Hula Valley in the north, where, with a graceful dip and glide, they came to a landing in the lush grassy marsh.

The Cranes greeted the storks, falcons, wagtails, pelicans, and other bird families that had gathered there. They exchanged honks, bellows, and whoops of joy. Everyone was having a wonderful time when Ima Crane looked up and around. "Oh no!" she gasped. "Where is Alexandra?"

The Cranes peered through papyrus and brambles. They poked their long heads through the reeds.

"Alexandra!" they shouted.

"There she is!" exclaimed Saba. Alexandra Crane, full of gangly grace, was performing before a group of crane chicks, frolicking and flapping joyously to a rhythm all her own.

About Israel's Bird Migration

Israel is known as a paradise for migrating birds. Twice each year, over five hundred million birds fly over Israel on their way to and from Asia, Europe, and Africa. During migrating season, pelicans, herons, storks, cranes and many other species flock to the Hula Valley where the birds rest, eat, and refuel before continuing on their journey. Bird watchers and bird lovers from all over the world come to marvel at this natural spectacle.

Photo by Aviran Avizedeq